For everyone

who ever waited for a cat to come in!

First U.S. edition 2019
First published as *Maya & Cat* by Walker Books Australia 2018

Library of Congress Catalog Card Number pending
ISBN 978-1-5362-0423-0

19 20 21 22 23 24 TLF 10 9 8 7 6 5 4 3 2 1

Printed in Dongguan, Guangdong, China

This book was typeset in Fnord Seventeen.
The illustrations were done in watercolor.

Candlewick Press
99 Dover Street
Somerville, Massachusetts 02144

visit us at www.candlewick.com

Maya and the Lost Cat

Caroline Magerl

CANDLEWICK PRESS

On a roof

as wet as a seal,

as gray as a puddle,

Cat was rumbling

a rumbly purr.

For feather boas,

she wouldn't come down . . .

nor pink shoelaces,

nor a pom-pom on a stick.

So Maya sent out a boatful of fish

with a tiny tin sail and waited

behind an open door.

Pad pad thump.
In perfectly quiet
fur boots,

Cat came to see —
and ate every
oily silver morsel!

Cat climbed high and

wrapped herself up in a soggy tail.

Maya watched her,

floating above

a thousand lit windows.

One window must be Cat's own.

Then — *pad pad thump.*

Maya placed a new can of fish
in her pocket and set out
to find Cat's home.

Cat followed politely behind.

Maya knocked on a door and asked,

"Do you belong to this cat?"

"No."

"Does this cat

belong to you?"

"No."

"Have you lost a cat?"
"Probably not."

Cat didn't blink once,

and she disappeared around a corner.

Maya plodded home,

where Cat was neatly seated in her bicycle basket.

This time Maya
followed Cat's nose.
Down through the town
and across the park.

Along the shore
and onto the pier, *thunketty thunk*
on the wooden boards.

Cat sprang

circus lion–style

as Fritz and Irma,

beaming and calling,

threw their arms

into the air.

Cat was home.
They celebrated with cookies
shaped like starfish.

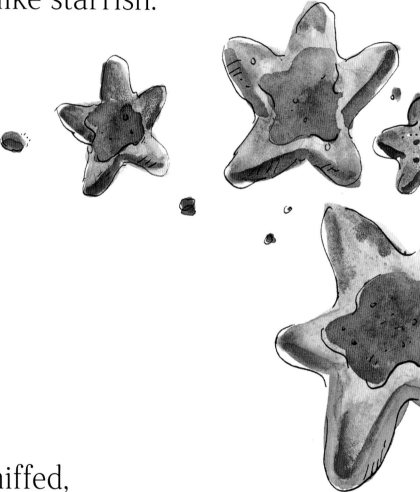

Maya sniffed,
just a little,
because she would miss Cat.

Then, sly and gentle,

Cat carried something . . .

a small and

cloudy gray bundle . . .

and gave her kitten
to Maya.

"Never seen
a kitty so seasick."
Fritz and Irma agreed.

Maya said goodbye

and rode home,

trying her best not to wobble.

That night,

the sky thundered

and the rain hosed down.

But in the waves and folds of Maya's blankets,

Moby purred a small and warm rumbly purr.